MW00953484

ISBN: 979-8-218-27576-1

Written by Brian Wolf
Illustrated by Alexandra Hombs

Printed in the United States of America.

This book is dedicated to all the School Resource Officers and D.A.R.E. Officers who spend their days protecting and teaching our kiddos. It takes a special kind of officer who is willing to partner up with teachers and parents to help make our children as successful as they can be in life.

Never forget you are a role model!

You have Courage
You had ACTION work!

THANK YOU
Officer Wolf
Prairie village
Police

No Touch please

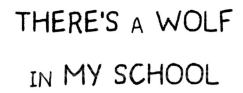

THERE'S A WOLF IN MY SCHOOL

Thank you!

Officer Wolf

my hero
Thank You

Officer Wolf is a GREAT COP!

Hi! My name is Brie.
I go to school at Village
Elementary. Every day since I
can remember, we have had
the bestest police officer ever
come to our school.

His name is Officer Wolf.
No he's not a real wolf but he is tall and has very spikey hair.
Besides having an awesome last name, he is very nice and always has a smile on his face. He does not howl at the moon or grow fur but he does wear a cool uniform with lots of shiny badges on it. His uniform even has stars on it!

So why is he the bestest you ask? Well...

First of all, he comes to our school every day in his cool police car.

He greets us at the door in the morning.

He always says "hi" in the hallway.

He helps us with our work.

He is always interested in our projects hanging in the hallway.

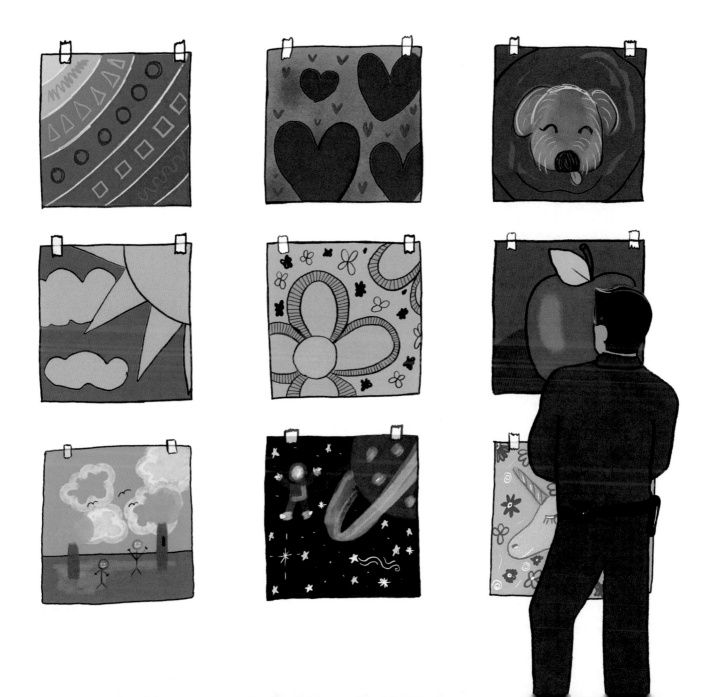

He helps out in the lunchroom — opens yogurt, peels bananas, tells us riddles, even uses the broom to help clean up.

One time, he brought his police friends to have lunch with us!

He plays with us at recess...
in his police uniform!

He comes to PE Class and plays games — sometimes he is on our team!

He tells great stories about...
bank robbers, his pets, animals he has dealt with while
working and people he took to jail for making bad choices.

He teaches us about his uniform and the equipment he carries.
One time I got to wear his handcuffs!
Would you believe he even has a pair of squirrel handcuffs?

He even lets us wear his sunglasses!
Well, sometimes...

He likes to ask us questions, too.

Are those new shoes?
Did you get your hair cut?
Did you paint your nails?

This one time, my girl scout troop went to the police station and Officer Wolf gave us a tour! He even showed us the jail cell!

He even comes to our sporting events over the weekend!

He teaches the younger students
how to safely ride their bikes.
I remember in second grade,
he taught my class ways to be safe...
I still remember the rules today!

And once every year, Officer Wolf helps with our school auction by offering to give one lucky student a ride to school in his awesome police car. He'll even bring breakfast to the house when he picks you up!

One day during summer break, he and his friends stopped to get lemonade!

I have even seen him directing traffic and giving tickets out!

Officer Wolf is so cool... on Halloween, there are at least 100 kids that dress up as him!

One time at the school carnival,
I saw Officer Wolf in the dunk tank!

My favorite classes are when he talks about why we follow the rules, always being kind and accepting of others, and of course The Golden Rule. Officer Wolf always tries to answer every one of our questions when he teaches our class.

The most important thing I learned was if
I ever need help, I can go to a police officer.

We love Officer Wolf and everything he does for us. Besides keeping us safe, he makes school and growing up fun!

I hope you get to meet an
Officer Wolf sometime... and soon!

THE END!

ABOUT OFFICER WOLF

Officer Wolf joined the Prairie Village Police Department in 2010. Since he was born and raised in the City of Prairie Village, the department was a natural fit. Very early in his law enforcement career, Officer Wolf expressed interest to work in the elementary schools teaching students the D.A.R.E. Program. In 2013, he got that opportunity. Officer Wolf remained in the elementary schools for seven years teaching students how to be safe, responsible and to make good choices. During those years, he created a new perception of what a police officer was. The students and families quickly realized he was someone they could trust and someone they could go to for help whenever the need arose. That trust quickly spread to law enforcement in general. More positive interactions began in the community and continue on into today. This book is a representation of Officer Wolf's time he spent in the schools and the positive impact he had.

Besides teaching the D.A.R.E. Program, Officer Wolf's Law Enforcement Career includes being a Field Training Officer, Member of the Hostage Negotiations Team, a Peer Support Team Member, a Recruitment Team Member and a CIT Officer. Recognition at the Department includes the Award of Valor and the Lifesaving Award. His current assignment is in the Patrol Division.

Officer Wolf is married and has two sons. When not spending time with the family, he likes to hunt, fish and is an avid soccer fan.

ABOUT THE ILLUSTRATOR

Kansas City based illustrator, Alexandra (Ali) Hombs, has made several children's books within the last few years. Graphic design and narrative illustration quickly became her main focus since graduating from Stephens College.

Ali is always striving to create something inspiring for little ones and adults alike.

Made in the USA
Monee, IL
13 November 2023

45947181R00021